THE
FOAL
IN THE
WIRE

THE FOAL IN THE WIRE

ROBBIE COBURN

LOTHIAN

A Lothian Children's Book

Published in Australia and New Zealand in 2025
by Hachette Australia
(an imprint of Hachette Australia Pty Limited)
Gadigal Country, Level 17, 207 Kent Street, Sydney, NSW 2000
www.hachettechildrens.com.au

Hachette Australia acknowledges and pays our respects to the past, present and
future Traditional Owners and Custodians of Country throughout Australia
and recognises the continuation of cultural, spiritual and educational practices
of Aboriginal and Torres Strait Islander peoples. Our head office is located on
the lands of the Gadigal people of the Eora Nation.

Copyright © Robbie Coburn 2025

This book is copyright. Apart from any fair dealing for the purposes of private study,
research, criticism or review permitted under the *Copyright Act 1968*, no part
may be stored or reproduced by any process without prior written permission.
Enquiries should be made to the publisher.

A catalogue record for this
book is available from the
National Library of Australia

ISBN: 978 0 7344 2360 3 (paperback)

Cover design by Christabella Designs
Cover illustration by Tannya Harricks
Author photo by Matt Coburn
Typeset in 12/17.5 pt Bembo MT Pro by Bookhouse, Sydney
Printed and bound in Australia by McPherson's Printing Group

The paper this book is printed on is certified against the
Forest Stewardship Council® Standards. McPherson's Printing
Group holds FSC® chain of custody certification SA-COC-005379.
FSC® promotes environmentally responsible, socially beneficial
and economically viable management of the world's forests.

For those who are wounded and surviving

WAITING
FOALS

FOAL

As I run down the veranda steps
in the dark
I can still hear them screaming
at each other
inside the house.

he doesn't love her
and she doesn't love him
but they stay.

I wish my words could change us,
teach our bodies to know
one another differently —

I want to teach him to love her
the way he can teach a horse to run
in the right direction.

I wish you could change
people's behaviour
like you can with a horse.

I know they blame me
for holding them
together here.
I try to be invisible.

as I walk down the path
towards the horse track
I notice the stillness of the farm
as their voices fade into the distance.
no sound but the wind
through the grasses of the paddocks
on every side.

on the farm's border, I see
there is a girl standing at the fence.
Julia.
the girl my age
from the next property.

we have spoken before
but in this darkness
our bodies are strangers.

Sam.
I can hear her call my name,
hear the ache of her voice
willing me towards her.

as I meet her eyes
at the paddock's edge
I see she is standing
over a wounded foal.

I can smell the blood
and hear the panicked breathing —

hers and my own
and the faltering breath
of the injured foal

tangled in barbed wire,
the trembling shape
of a body in the grass.

CUTTING WIRE

Pressing my foot on the lowest wire
of the fence
I make a space for my body
and climb through
to the other side,
careful the wire doesn't
burrow further
into the foal's flesh.

it's caught.
we have to cut the wire.

Julia turns and moves
through the dark grass
of the paddock
towards a shed
in the distance.

alone with the foal,
I lie down beside it

and run my hand gently
across its neck.

there are small furrows
caked with dried blood
where the barbs
have pierced the skin.

the foal raises its head slightly
and looks at me, confused.

I can see the pain welling up
behind its eyes.

I rest my head
on its flank
and feel its laboured breathing,

I hover my fingers over
the open wounds
and wish I could give the foal
my body.

I won't let anybody hurt you.

*you can't hurt a body
that is beyond reach.*

Julia returns
with the wire-cutters.

*Do you think it was waiting for us?
I've never seen it before.*

the foal must have broken
into the paddock
from one of the
neighbouring properties
in the distance.

I haven't seen it before either —
I wonder how far it must have stumbled
to find itself here.

a dam would never leave her foal alone.
it must have walked off and become lost
taking a narrow path
somehow
its mother couldn't follow.

I hope our parents will think
the wire was torn
by a cow breaking
through the fence.

I remove my jacket
and lay it on the grass,
pushing it beneath
the foal's body.

it stirs slightly
when I reach across its back
and feel the cold wire
against my palms
as I wrap my hands
around it.

Julia cuts the wire
and I slowly lift it
from the foal's neck.

we roll the fragile creature over
until its body rests
on the jacket.

we take one side
of the jacket each
and together we pull
the wounded animal free.

EUTHANASIA

I had seen it before —
a wounded animal
staring,
bewildered, down the barrel of dad's rifle

the piercing shock of the bullet
driving into its skin
and entering the temple
before it fell
against the earth.

the foal is just a baby.

as kids we were told
that once a horse's legs break
the pain is too much
for them to live with
and they usually never get better.

dad said horses didn't know
what it meant to be born or to die.
that there was no fear.

only a horse's body aches.

I didn't believe him.
I could see in their eyes
that they know sadness
the way we do.

no one tries desperately
to survive
if they don't fear leaving.

and they missed each other
the way we would
if one of us left.

the way the paddocks
fell silent
when the other animals heard the shot
and knew someone had died.

I tell Julia about the bodies
of horses
dad has buried on the farm.
she says they are everywhere
beneath her on their side
of the fence too.

she starts to cry
as she stands over
the trembling creature
noticing the confused, fearful eyes
and I wrap my arms
around her body gently.

only a horse's body aches.

back then, dad had told us to stop crying
and pretend the horse was sleeping.

and I would have been able to
were it not for the blood

running across its forehead
and filling its glazed eye.

CREEK HOUSE

There is no sound
but the foal's tortured breathing
and a soft rain that has begun
to fall against
our hair and faces.

we slowly drag the foal's body
on the jacket
through the grass
towards the centre
of the paddock.

Julia stops and gestures
to a dark opening
in the earth

and I see that it is
an empty creek.

the foal will be safe here.

the creek is forty acres
from Julia's house
and she says her dad never
comes here anymore.

I step down carefully
onto the eroded dirt and rocks.

Julia takes one side of the jacket
and I take the other,
lifting the wounded body
from the earth
and slowly lowering it down.

the foal feels heavy
as it falls into my arms
and against my chest.

it makes no sound
but I can feel its breath
against my skin
and smell the panic
escaping from its coat.

Julia takes a small torch from her pocket —
inside the creek
are rusted, burnt-out cars
and other parts
separated from their bodies.

engines the colour
of horse manure
that melt into
the dark landscape.

doors, windows, wheels.

seats torn open
and crawling with insects.

there is the shell
of an old Ford model
resting against one of the banks,
missing its interior,

only a cracked roof
and a space
where one of the back doors
had once been.

we pull the foal inside
and let it rest
underneath the roof.

we stand on either side
of its body
and as we sit down
our faces almost touch.

I watch its chest rise and fall,
I notice the area
between its legs.

the foal is a colt.

I can hear the rain
beginning
to fall harder against
the metal roof
above our heads.

no more pain.
no more blood.
no more wire.

only the safety
of this abandoned shell
protecting the foal
from the night.

we can be invisible here.

WAKING FOAL

The foal seems to be coming back.

the delirium caused by the wounds
and exposure while he lay
in the paddock, tangled in wire,
seems to be fading
and he is slowly taking in
his surroundings.

here in the creek
with Julia and I,

he looks at us,
confused and afraid.

I wish we could tell him
that we won't hurt him
and only want to help.

he can't tell us
what he is thinking

but as he looks into our faces,
the urgency in his eyes
is continually asking,

who are you?
why am I here?

SCREAMS

Sometimes, I stand in a paddock
and hear screaming
all around me.

I know she must
hear it too.

I have known Julia
since we were kids
but once we started to grow up
we never spent time together

some days I see her waiting
for the bus or sitting
on the oval at school
and we both turn
and smile at each other,
but I am never brave enough
to speak to her.

at least not before
we found the injured foal
caught in the wire.

her mum isn't around
and her dad drinks too much.

sometimes, when I'm walking
the paddocks at night,
I can hear the piercing cry
of his voice in the distance
or the sound of something
breaking.

in the darkness,
and so far from our houses,
it almost sounds
like he is competing
with my parents to scream
the loudest.

I imagine they are talking
to each other

and that my parents
are a team, arguing with him
instead of amongst themselves.

Julia walks beside me
as we approach
the barbed-wire fence
that separates
our properties.

the tangled wires
lying in the grass
from where the fence was cut
create an opening
that makes it feel
like we are no longer apart
and live on one big farm.

you go home.
I can come straight back.
dad won't be looking for me.

I will bring the foal
water and some formula
in a bottle from dad's shed.

*I've seen him use it with foals before.
and I'll bring a blanket.*

*I'll make sure he gets up
and walks a little bit
so he isn't laying down too long.
we don't want him getting sores
on his sides.*

we have to keep him moving.

*I'll leave some soaked pellets
and hay for him too,
so he will have food
while we are gone.*

*let's meet here tomorrow night.
be at the fence
at the same time.*

after we say goodbye
and promise to come back
the next night,
I climb through the broken fence
and begin walking back
towards the house.

I already want
to see her face again.

without thinking, I look back
to see Julia turning,

and our eyes meet.

BROTHER

My brother died in the practice pen
after being thrown and stomped on
by a bull.
there was nothing glorious about it,
no arena or cheering crowd

just his body lying motionless in the dirt,
the wind heaping clouds of dust
across his back and hat.

I watched him become a ghost
before I ran back to the house,
screaming.

dad, he's not moving.
he isn't getting back up.

ONLY CHILD

I am always alone in this house,
even when my parents are here.
the farm feels empty.
after my brother died, I couldn't bear
to go to the yard
where he was killed anymore,
making a path through the property,
unable to even look at anything
that reminded me of him.
I feel disconnected and lost, a child
walking aimlessly in the silence
of endless paddocks.
sometimes I feel like
the only person in the world.

HEALING COLT

In the morning light, the glare of the sun
moves its way through the branches
of a big gum tree in the centre of
the horse track in the back paddock.

it is a warm day and my parents
are at the races.
they are at the races most Saturdays
and now I'm older
they don't make me go with them.

I think about Julia
as I walk out into the paddock
and how we will go and visit
the foal together after nightfall
as we promised we would.
I lie in the grass and imagine
I am the foal getting better.

HOW TO SHRINK

Photographs of horse races
line the walls of the lounge room
in our weatherboard house.

in the corner of each of them
there is a photo of my dad
standing next to the winning
horse and driver.
sometimes my mum is there too.

there are even some
with my older brother in them
from back when he was alive.

my only friend at school, Alex,
always makes fun of our house
and the way it doesn't look like
other people's.

that it is so small
and we don't have
the nice things that his parents do.
he makes fun of my clothes
and the food mum makes me
that I bring to school for lunch.

he tells me
I should be embarrassed
that my parents are poor
and says we are bogans
for racing horses.

he says my brother
is lucky he died
so he doesn't
have to be embarrassed
by me and my family anymore.

he knows how much this harms me
but is certain I will stay.

I'm too scared to bring anyone
else over to the house
for fear they will laugh at me too,

so I can't make
any other friends at school.

Alex says I am lucky
he is kind enough
to hang around me,
even though I am a loser.

I wonder if Julia is my friend now,
and if Alex would make fun of her too.
when I told her about our place,
she said her house was the same,
maybe even smaller,
and her dad has even more
horse photos
lining the walls of his shed.

Alex teaches me
that I am not enough,
and won't ever be.

he teaches me how to shrink.

THINKING

All day I think about dying.

there are cows everywhere
across the paddock
but they don't go down
into the creek
because they won't be able
to climb back out again.

I think about going down there
and never coming back up.

THE KELLY GANG

I remember when we were children —
sometimes on the weekend
I would go to Alex's house
and we would pretend
we were bushrangers
running around his property.

we marked off an area
with fallen branches
in one of the paddocks
and made-believe it was
the Glenrowan Hotel.

we wore helmets
made out of papier-mâché
and held toy guns we silently
fired into the air.

we made shooting sounds
with our voices,
imagining we were in a shootout.

Alex was always Ned Kelly
and I was never allowed to be.
I had to be one of the other
members of the Kelly Gang

but it was fun and he wasn't mean
unless he thought I was making it
look like he wasn't the leader.

I always had to fall down
at the end
and pretend I had died
during the conflict,
while he screamed
and pretended he had been captured.

he was the hero
and I was only his sidekick

but I got lost in pretending
and forgot about everything

like smoke escaping from
the chimney of our house
in winter
and disappearing
into the pale sky.

FURTIVE

dad wakes early to work the horses
and mum wakes up when she hears him
fumbling for his clothes in the dark,
walking through the front door
and across the veranda.
she counts the steps as he walks
down them,
across the car bay
and out into the shed.

when it gets dark
mum goes and reads in bed
and dad falls asleep on the couch
watching the races.

at night, they both go to sleep early
so they don't hear me get out of bed
and slide my bedroom window open,
climbing down and landing on the grass
then stepping down the path

making sure to stay on the clover
lining the sides of the path
to avoid the potholes and depressions
left in the ground by horses.

I am careful mum and dad don't hear me
when I hoist myself back up
through the window
and onto the bed
when I return.

I can't make any noise.

it is always so quiet out here at night
that the smallest misstep could disturb
the silence and wake them.

they don't suspect anything.

DARK

At night,
I hear dad turn over
on the couch
in the lounge room

and the creak of the springs
as they move
beneath his weight.

me and dad don't talk much
and I feel like
he doesn't know me.

not the way he knew my brother.

he loved him and said
he was the great hope
for his children
carrying on his legacy
and preserving the farm.

dad said he always thought
one day my brother
would take over the property.

I lie back and stare at the ceiling.
hearing silence from my brother's
empty bedroom —

I want to walk out there
and ask dad if he wishes
I had died instead.

GHOSTS

*I think dad drinks because he is trying
to outrun a memory,* Julia says.

*I hate the way he treats me
but I know he is in pain
and haunted by the way she left.*

*he told me that before she went away,
she swallowed a bottle of pills
and had to be taken
to hospital.*

*right before
she left us for good.*

I look at her, searching her face
for a sign to comfort her,
or say something that will help.

the light from the moon
seems to frame her face
as her hair blows slightly
over her shoulders.

there's only the two of us,
and the foal
down here in the creek.

our parents are in the houses,
seemingly miles away.

Julia thinks that when
we lose someone,
they are still always following us
and that's why we can't
let go and move on.

*I try to imagine what my mum
would look like now*, Julia says.

*sometimes when I look at myself
in the mirror
I imagine I am staring into her eyes
and begging her to return.*

STAY

It is hard to be friends
with Alex
but I can't imagine leaving

because we have been friends
since we were kids.

sometimes he is kind to me
and I think he has changed,
until he says something
that makes me feel small again.

I wonder if it is a game,
and he pretends to be nice
only so he can tear me
down again.

whenever I try to talk
to Julia at school,
he interferes

and tells me
I shouldn't talk to her.

Julia says I need to
stand up for myself
and that I don't need him
because I have her,

a friend who won't
make me feel like this.

it's ok, I say.
he is my friend.

but I always think about dying
and how I want the ache
in my head to stop.

I plan on walking out
into the paddocks one day
and not stopping

until I disappear.
instead, I think of the foal
and how he will need me
tomorrow.

FEAR

Julia.

even the sound of her name
as it rolls off my tongue
pulses beneath my breath
and electrifies my skin.

we sit in the creek bed,
taking turns feeding
the colt pellets
we have soaked in water
to make it easier
for him to swallow.

we help him
stagger to his feet
again.

we have to keep him moving.

I want to tell her there is more here
than a friendship
bound in our care for the foal

but when I reach out
to hold her hand,
she pulls away.

I feel the fear in my body
as I start to shake gently.

Julia tells me she is scared
to get close to anyone
because of her mum

and says that everyone leaves.

if you never let anyone
get too close and know you
then you won't have
to miss them.

like the foal, she is afraid of my touch.

things have to move slowly.

Julia.

I promise you

I'm not going anywhere.

RAIN

It is raining heavily,
but I climb through the window
and carefully make my way
down the path.

Julia isn't at the fence,
but I know she will be
taking shelter in the creek.

I find her with the foal,
wrapped in the blanket
beneath the car roof.

she is stroking his mane softly
and feeding him pellets from
the palm of her hand.

Julia is kind to the foal,
and to me.

the foal is kind to us too,
slowly trusting us
and letting us get closer.

night after night I notice the foal's body
getting stronger.

I pour small amounts
of ointments and creams
from the shed
into empty water bottles
so dad won't notice
anything missing,
and take them down
with me to the creek.

I run the cream along the wounds
covering the colt's neck
as Julia watches me, smiling.

when he brays softly,
she rests her head against his.

you're beautiful, she says to me.

*you can trust people
who are kind to animals.
not like my dad.*

I tell her my brother was like that
and would never harm an animal

if you care for an animal, he said,
*they will care for you too,
even save you.*

we all need to take care of each other.

I run my hand over Julia's shoulder gently
as she brushes the foal's hair.

I feel a warmth come over my body
and the rain doesn't matter.

WAITING

Night.
we meet at the paddock's edge
before I climb the fence
and we cross the paddock
towards the creek.

we both know how to feed
and care for foals
as we have watched our dads do
so many times.

Julia has brought another bottle of formula
and I have a bundle of hay
I gathered
from inside the shed.

dad won't notice.
whenever hay is lifted,
stalks fall from the bale
and gather on the floor.

that day I had seen dad
mending the fence.

I have been waiting nervously
to see Julia again.
I am wearing one of my best shirts
and I combed my hair
before walking outside.

I wonder if Julia has been waiting
to see me
and if the foal has been waiting
for us.

the foal is lying on his side
beneath the car's shell,
covered in a blanket.

Julia hands me the bottle of formula.

I place the teat in the foal's mouth
and he drinks.

I lay the bundle of hay on the earth
and watch as he licks at the stalks,
and chews, swallowing quickly.

I reach out and hold Julia's hand
and feel the pressure of her
gripping mine back.

the foal looks at us.
we will never know how he
found himself that way,

wounded, trapped and alone.

he won't survive without us.

maybe we were all waiting
to find each other.

BUTTERFLY

After we leave the foal, we walk
across the paddock
and stand together at the fence.
I tell Julia I will see her
back here tomorrow night
and we agree the foal looks better.
we talk about school and our parents
but she is so beautiful to me
that I can't think of anything else.

BLAME

Almost every night I hear them fighting.
mum blames dad for my brother
riding bulls in the first place.
dad says he told him not to.

Mum thinks my brother was trying
to be tougher than my dad
and prove something
and the way dad treated us as kids
is the reason we do the things we do.

I know it doesn't matter
because he isn't coming back

and no amount of screaming
will change that.

QUESTIONING

Some nights, I wonder
why I hear screams
coming from Julia's house
when her mum isn't there.

I wonder if Julia is listening
to her dad
fight with himself.

APERTURE

Ever since my brother died,
my mind doesn't feel
like it belongs to me.

he rode bulls and bucking horses
at rodeos all over the state
and his dream was to be
the Australian champion.

my parents were proud of him
but dad thinks bull riders
are insane.

he said you don't have to be crazy
to ride them, but it helps.

my brother was only seventeen
when he died.

I tell Julia it happened
four years ago
but it still hurts.

sometimes, I have a dream
where he is lying in the dirt
of the practice pen, asleep,
and there is a bull charging
towards him at the other end.

I try to shake him awake
but he doesn't move
until the bull's horns
drive into his back
and I disappear
from the frame.

for some reason, I feel safe
telling Julia about him
and my dreams.
things I could never tell Alex
and have always hidden
from everyone.

I trust you.
I haven't felt ok since he left
and my parents started fighting.
I know they wish I wasn't around.
I think everyone would be better off
if I wasn't here.

sometimes I think I am going crazy.
maybe I should ride a bull.

my voice trembles
when I tell Julia
that I think about leaving
this place.

not just this farm,
but everywhere.

Kiss

The first time I kiss Julia
I forget about the foal.
I see the wind blow through her hair
and the night disappear.
it feels like there is something opening
in the pit of my stomach,
a widening space that will constantly
be filling itself with her name.
for the first time, I understand
what people mean
when they say they are in love.

RETALIATION

Alex sees me talking to Julia
after school.

what are you doing talking to her?
you don't talk to her.
she's just your weird neighbour
with the drunk dad.

I want to scream
and tell him to stop
but I just say that sometimes
I spend time with Julia
on the farm at night
and we catch
the school bus together.

he laughs and says
we must have a lot in common
because we are both poor.

Julia tells him to shut up
and leave us alone.

Alex doesn't like it when people
stand up for themselves.

no wonder your mother left.
you're just the daughter
of a drunk.
you'll be just like her.
you probably already are.

when I punch him,
the anguish of every time
he has hurt me
drives into his jaw.

my fist is bleeding
but I don't notice
as I look back at Julia and smile.

it feels like I'm someone else.

FIRST TIME

I have never felt a fear
that consumes me this way,
but I don't want it to be
with anyone but her.

the world has already disappeared
before our lips touch
and I feel her press against me.

as we take off our clothes,
her beauty piercing my eyes
so intensely
that I can see her smiling
even when I close them.

there is a calming safety in her arms,
her cold fingertips tracing
my neck and spine
when she tells me she is ready.

in this first moment
we both tremble
as if we share the same body.

it shouldn't hurt when you
love someone.

it doesn't feel wrong
or the way
the boys at school
said it would

but like a closeness beyond skin
as if you could see a human heart
beating in front of your eyes
and hold it against your own.

I know it is not enough
to love a body.

I want to love every inch of her
that I have never seen before now
and those I can never see,

the parts of her I can only ever
reach with my mind

like holding a body
and cradling a ghost
at the same time.

WALKING

The foal is walking around the creek bed
leaving the imprints of his tiny hoofs
in the dry earth.

he stops in front of Julia and she runs
her hand across the short hair of his mane.
he lies back down on the ground
then rolls onto his feet, pressing them
into the earth and stumbling
as if he were being born again feet-first,
gazing all around as if
seeing the world for the first time.

we walk beside him, stepping awkwardly
around the old car parts beneath our feet
as if we are learning to walk again.

I can still see the foal's body
tangled in the wire

when I touch the lacerations
covering his neck

but they are now closed and fading.

maybe scars can heal if we give them
a chance to
and survival is possible
if we aren't alone.

I tell Julia that
I don't want to die anymore.

COMPOSURE

Every day at school between classes
I spend my time with Julia now.

we sit together on the bus
and only leave one another
when we have to.

every night when it gets dark
I leave the house and meet her
at the fence at the back of the property.

we feed and water the foal
and tell each other things
we have never told anyone.

Alex leaves me alone now.
Julia thinks he is scared of me.

sometimes we kiss
on the oval at lunchtime
and don't care if anyone sees.

TEENAGER

The earth was a box
made of glass.

the kitten learned how to sleep
in the greyhound's jaws.

when I dug a hole
in the shape of my body
but left it empty

you couldn't hurt me anymore.

MERCY HORSES

SLEEPING HORSE

Did you know that the fully grown horse
often sleeps standing up
because to lie down too long
can mean its death?
their blood flow
becomes restricted
and causes excess pressure
on their organs —
they don't know why they wake
in the night and stand up
but they do.
not like you
who is unmoving in the cold
and empty bedroom.
imagine being able to decide
to lie down
and fall asleep forever.

LOVE

When she first called my name,
it felt like her voice was pressing itself
into my skin.

meeting her properly
for the first time
and immediately knowing her
turned the words into a pair of hands.

her family's farm
on the next property
where the road forks
into the world beyond our lives.

I wish I had not wasted
so many years of my life
not loving her.

searching for her,
I knew
I would only ever stop searching
to meet her gaze.

GROWING

The foal raises his head
and looks at us
when we arrive at the creek.
he doesn't look scared anymore
and seems to recognise us.
we watch as he slowly gets to his feet
again, and staggers forward,
drinking the milk and eating the hay.

we sit on one of the banks
and Julia tells me that sometimes
she doesn't know
when people are mistreating her
and thinks people
are mistreating her sometimes
when they're not.

*I don't trust anyone
other than you.*

I ask her if she thinks everything begins
when we are children
and if we spend the rest of our lives
not knowing how to connect
or why we react to things the way we do.

I wonder if my brother dying
is why I am scared of people leaving
and let Alex treat me the way he did.

and if her dad is why she is afraid
of everyone.

we both assume everyone
wants to hurt us
and let people treat us badly.

I want to hold Julia and tell her
it isn't her fault
and that I understand.

it's not our fault
we don't know how
to be treated properly.

I wrap my arms around her
and tell her everything will be ok

but I don't know if it will.

MERCY HORSE

Not all living things want to live.

the tree cannot cut itself down.

rain can be promised,
sunlight burrowing

into the body of the earth
where we buried my brother —

after he was cut down
before he could grow

like a seedling
trampled by horses.

NIGHTMARE

I believed it was real —
when I woke up crying
at three in the morning
after dreaming Julia's dad
cornered a prematurely born foal
and crushed it under his feet.

TWO SCREAMS

I arrive at the creek
and Julia isn't there.

I can hear screaming
coming from her house
in the distance.

two screams.

her dad's
and a higher-pitched, female voice.
then the sound of glass breaking.

Julia.

I run towards the house
and hear her father's voice
bellowing at her inside.

he is throwing empty beer bottles
against the walls
and watching as they shatter
and the broken glass
gathers beneath his feet.

the veranda creaks beneath
the weight of my footsteps
as I run through the door
and see Julia lying on the floor,
her father standing over her.

his boots drive into her stomach
and I watch his hand
come down hard
against her face

don't touch her.

I feel the collision of my fist
against the back of his skull
before I know what I have done.

he turns and strikes me suddenly
and I fall to the floor beside Julia.

keep her.
she's weak like her mother.

I try to get to my feet
to punch him again
but he pushes me back down.

the skin of his face is bright red
and looks like it's cooking
against his bones

and I can see saliva pooling
at the corners of his mouth.

his eyes look like the surface
of a dam beneath the moon.

I touch Julia's cheeks
and can feel the heat
burn beneath her skin
from the force
of her father's hands.

I kiss her and take hold
of both of her hands in mine.

slowly we get to our feet
and make our way
towards the door.

suddenly there is the sound of glass
shattering against the walls again
and we begin to run
out through the paddocks
towards the creek.

we can hear her father's screams
and the sound of bottles breaking
getting further away.

the foal is sleeping beneath
the roof of the car shell
when we make our way down
and sit silently on the eroded earth.

the night is still
and there is now only the hum
of crickets sounding
across the paddock.

Julia cries and talks
about leaving this place.

says her dad does this
every time he drinks too much
and starts talking about her mother.

he says Julia reminds him of her
the older she gets
and he can't stand the sight of her.

it is her fault her mum left
and that he can't stop drinking.

she doesn't feel safe here.

I tell Julia I love her
and hold her hand.

she tells me about her mum
and how she left
when she got tired of her dad hitting her
all the time when he was drunk.
he was always drunk back then too.

one morning when Julia was five
she woke to find the front door open
and her dad sitting at the table
with a bottle of whiskey and his rifle.

when she asked him where her mum was
he got to his feet,
taking her hand roughly
and hurriedly leading her outside
to a paddock near the house
where a mare had birthed a foal
that morning.

this filly will be useless
like your mother
and eat and drink all my money.

I'll show you how we fix it.

I squeeze her hand tighter
when she tells me

about the way she had covered her mouth
and screamed into her hand
until her palm was swollen

as she watched him take up his rifle
and drive a bullet
through the newborn foal's skull.

SEARCH

My body feels like it is
made of panic —

I run across the train platform
and away from the station,
my throat and legs aching.

I don't stop until I reach the right
building and go inside,
almost colliding
with the glass door as it opens.

the hospital feels empty
despite the bodies passing
me as I run down the corridors.

as if I can feel her somehow
inside the endless white walls
and worried faces
and our hands could touch

if I could just walk through
the right door.

after she swallowed the pills
her dad was too drunk to drive her
so she called
the ambulance herself.

it feels as if she isn't
anywhere.

if I cannot be with her
I want the hospital floor
to swallow me
so we can at least be
in the same place.

I can't find her
but my body won't let me turn
to go back home.

back to the waiting foal
and the world
that is just ours.

I don't want any world
without Julia.

RETURNING AND LEAVING

I wait by the window all morning
watching cars pass by the front fence,
travelling down the road
towards Julia's place.

at lunchtime, a white sedan drives past
the front gate and stops
before entering their property.

it's not her dad's ute
and I can tell something is wrong.

I watch the car progress
down the driveway behind the trees
until all I see is the dust
it throws up behind it
as it reaches the car bay

beneath an old shed
beside the house.

I stay there all afternoon at the window
watching the cars go by,
waiting for nightfall.

I can't eat or think of anything but Julia
walking back into that house
with her dad and the room
where she tried to vanish forever.

when it gets dark I run out to the fence
at the back of the property

and wait for what feels like forever.

then, I see her walking towards me
in the distance, smiling.

she looks sick but she is still
the most beautiful girl in the world.

she throws herself into my arms
and kisses me.

she tells me she is ok and that she is sorry
for what she did.
she says she only wanted to stop thinking
for a while.

the people at the hospital had put a tube
down her throat and drawn up the pills
out of her stomach.
they said she almost didn't make it.

she tells me they knew about her dad
once they saw the marks covering her skin.
they said she can't stay
with her dad anymore
and has to go and live with relatives
in another town, far away.

they have only let her come home
to gather her things.

her dad isn't here
and there is a woman who has come
to look after her
and will take her away again tomorrow.

I hope they will take her somewhere
better than this.

come with me.
we can start again.

I tell Julia I have to stay here
to look after the foal.

when I tell her I don't want her to leave,
the world has already become a wound
that swallows my body.

it is quiet
and I feel something
unnameable breaking
but I don't want her to see.

I don't want to make this harder for her.

she holds my hand.

I love you.

I love you.

we don't say anything else.

we just hold each other
for what feels like hours
that disappear in an instant.

I don't want to have to imagine
this paddock without Julia in it.

I can see everything
and wish I could cover my eyes.

I wish I was still sitting
by the front window,
watching the cars drive by

so I wouldn't know
she is coming back home
but not staying.

WOUNDED ANIMALS

TALK

mum and dad have stopped screaming
at each other.

they sit me down in the lounge room
and tell me they need to be apart
so they can stop fighting.

sometimes wounded people need space
and to be alone so they can heal.

they want to talk about my brother
and what has happened to them
so maybe they can love
one another again.

for now, mum is leaving
but I know it is better this way.

FAMILY PORTRAIT

The sky is clear
and the grey clouds
I can see in the distance
look like they are melting away
into the morning air.

soon only blue
will be left.

mum's voice calls me outside
where she's standing
in the car bay.

I notice she hasn't taken
all of her things from the house
which makes me think
she isn't leaving forever.

Sam.
here.
make sure you keep this.

mum hands me a photograph.

it shows her, dad, and my brother
and I as kids,
sitting on a fallen log in a paddock,
all together and smiling.

she tells me she loves me
and she will still be seeing me
as much as possible.

she hugs me
and I hold her back
as tightly as I can.

it can't be like this again, she says.
but it can still be ok.

TELLING

One morning, I lead my dad
over the back fence,
through the paddock
and down into the creek.

I want somebody to know

about how we found the foal,
tangled in the wire and wounded,
and how each night
we have nursed him back to health.

about Julia and her dad
and the night I saw him
standing over her body.

I begin to tell him
I know what happens
to sick foals who won't grow up
to run with the other horses.

this one has fight.
they don't all make it
but this one will because of you two.

he smiles and tells me
he is proud of me
and that the foal can stay with us.

he also tells me he is glad I am here
on the farm with him.

for the first time I don't just see him
as my dad
but as someone trying to make sense
of everything in his life.

I realise he is wounded like me

but doesn't know
how to tell anyone.

I tell him I love him
and want us to be closer.

suddenly, he hugs me

and we stay down there
in the creek with the foal
for a long time.

RUNNING FOAL

Inside the shed, I slowly lower a halter
onto the foal's head.
he pulls back suddenly
as I run my hand over his neck.

it's ok.
you can trust me.
we are going for a run.

I ease the halter onto him,
holding a carrot beneath his chin
and watching him chew
and swallow it within seconds.

clipping a lead to the halter,
I lead him outside,
down the path.

he walks slowly behind me,
not pulling or resisting.

we reach a paddock surrounding
a large dam
a mare and two geldings
lift their heads from their grazing
and stare at us when they hear
the iron gate open.

I lead him into the paddock
and unclip the lead from the halter.

go.
run.
you made it.

he stands beside me for a moment,
looking back as if to ask me
if everything is ok.
he hasn't been out here before like this.

I watch as he canters
into the centre of the paddock,
joining the others.

watching him run this way,
a foal I remember, wounded and afraid,
now healthy and grazing contentedly

amongst other horses,
causes a strange feeling to sink
into my body.

I don't feel sad
or wish that things were different.

myself, Julia, and the foal
aren't who we were before.

I feel like I'm letting go
of something.

NAMES

We never gave the foal a name.
it would have meant it existed
beyond the hidden world
of the creek.

everybody needs a name.

dad talks to me
about my older brother
for the first time I can remember
without mentioning him dying.

he tells me how good he was
with the horses

and that he liked to help the ones
who were sick or injured.

I imagine he has only gone away
like Julia

and can somehow hear
me and dad talking about him.

maybe a body can be with you
even if you can't see or touch it.

we give the foal my brother's name.

LETTER

At the entrance of the driveway
we have an old milk drum
impaled on a fence post
for a letterbox.

every day I have been stopping
and staring into its dark mouth
to see what's inside.

I have been spending time with dad
and the foal.
the foal is getting better
at walking by himself
and spending time
with the other horses.

sometimes dad asks me about Julia
and I tell him I think
it's better that she left
but I don't mean it.

when I notice the letter
one afternoon after school,
scrawled with my name and address,
I already know it's from her.

I open the envelope,
unfolding the note
and running my hands
over the paper
as if it were on fire.

Dear Sam.
how are you feeling?
I am living with my aunty
and uncle on the coast.
there is a school here
that they've let me into and I've made a friend.
she doesn't know anything about farms or horses
and her parents travel a lot for work
but she treats me better than everyone did back
*   home.*
it's funny. even though I'm not from here
I feel like I blend in better
than I did where I come from.
maybe home can be anywhere you want it to be.

*maybe a place is your home
when it feels like it's your home.*

*my aunty took me to talk to someone,
to speak about what happened with dad,
and my mum not being around.
then she took me to the doctor
and they gave me tablets to help me feel better.
I think they're working.*

*I don't feel so sad all the time anymore.
but there's no one here like you.
I feel better but I feel sad
that I'm not with you.
I think about you every day
and wonder if you are ok.
I wonder if the foal is ok too.
sometimes it feels like you're here
when I close my eyes.
especially at night.
I miss you.
love Julia.*

I fold the letter and close my eyes,
imagining Julia's face brushing

against mine as I wrap
my arms around her again.

then the unbearable absence
of her body as she pulls away.

it feels like the words
are carving themselves
into me somewhere,
taking something before
I realise I have lost it.

she isn't coming back.

AFTER

Nobody knows what we have seen and felt
inside our houses, hidden behind trees,
in dry creek beds and in dark paddocks.

only we know what we carry with us
when our bodies change
and we find ourselves somewhere new
as somebody else.

everything is temporary.
everything will change.

in the distance
the light you will never see
if you don't stay and wait for it.

I don't know what I will do
after I leave school and the farm,
but I want to write about what happened.
I want to write down everything

about my brother and Julia and the foal.

I am no longer ashamed of who I am
and where I come from.

I can hold on and be anyone.

LETTING GO

One day the creek
filled with rain
and washed away
our footprints.

the foal's tiny hoofmarks,
carved into the dry earth,
filled with water
and vanished.

I still walk
through the paddocks
towards it,
expecting to see her
standing at the fence,
smiling.

in the fading light
the words for forgetting
are like burning leaves
as they fall against her hair,

dreaming that one night
she will be here
holding my body again
and reminding me to stay.

you mark anything you touch
in this world.

our footsteps disappearing
doesn't mean we didn't
walk here.

I feel the warmth of her fingers
between mine
as she walks across the paddock
beside me
releasing my hand
as she climbs down
into the creek.

I realise the act
of letting go of her hand
is the same as taking it
in reverse.

WOUNDED ANIMAL

You can create a life
out of fear,
but you don't have to.

sometimes,
in the lightless room,
it feels like the sky
never existed

and the horses
have stopped running,

even the mare
who continually
tried to run

when you were a child;

a loose nail on a fence post
the horses had kicked loose

drove into her leg
and tore her fetlock,

the blood
causing her white sock
to turn red and pool
on her hoof.

she picked at the wound
each day,

tearing at the scab
as if to make the reality
of her injury untrue —

attempting to run
with the others,

the blood
forming patches
in the grass
for you to find

as you followed her.

and to finally see
this now
and what has become
of your life —
your skin will never
understand
the ache in your mind,
even if you try
to teach it.

like that mare
who only ever thought
to run again,

maybe this
scarred and haunted body
is enough —

the wounded animal
is capable of survival.

ACKNOWLEDGEMENTS

There are not adequate words for me to express my gratitude to those who helped make this book happen, but I will try to do you all justice. None of this would have been possible without all of you. This is our book. May our foal run forever.

My publisher, Jeanmarie Morosin, who believed in this story immediately and made my childhood dream come true – I wish there was a way to articulate how lucky and thankful I feel to have worked on this book with you. I cannot ever thank you enough and I will always be so proud of what we have made.

Karen Ward, for being an editor extraordinaire and doing so much to bring this book to life.

Deonie Fiford, for the best copyedit any writer could hope for, that truly helped tie up the loose ends.

Tannya Harricks, for creating the most beautiful cover artwork I have ever seen – you are such an extraordinary artist and having your work on the book cover was meant to be and a dream come true.

Ron Koertge, Sonya Hartnett, Steven Herrick, Sharon Kernot and Louis Nowra, for their kind support and endorsements – you are all huge heroes of mine, and I still can't believe this is real. I will always cherish your words.

Jeanne Ryckmans, who has helped me more than words can say – without you, none of this would have happened. You are the greatest agent in the world, but more importantly, one of the most beautiful human beings in the world. I hope you always know how loved and appreciated you are and that you make the world so much brighter for so many people.

Belinda Bolliger at Key People Literary Management, who first put me on the path to write a verse novel and supported and inspired me all the way through the writing of this story and beyond – you are the reason any of this was possible and I won't ever forget that. There are certain people you cross paths with who change the entire trajectory of your life and make you feel that the universe is looking out for you. Saying thank you isn't enough.

My dear friends Michele Seminara, Candida Baker, Judith Beveridge, Timothy Lee, Lou Verga, Claire Miranda Roberts, Amanda Anastasi, Dimitra Harvey, Anne Walsh, Luke Best, Emily Butcher, Joe Rullo, Leanne Neill, David Rankine, Josh Grech, and Kaylen Court – no matter what has happened in the past, I know what true friendship and mutual respect and kindness is because of you.

Shelby Morgan, who supported and believed in me all along, especially throughout the writing of this book. I wouldn't be here without you.

The poets and writers who have saved and sustained me and been some of my closest companions – most of you won't ever know, but this book wouldn't exist without you.

The editors and publishers who have believed in my poetry over the years and helped me find my way along this crooked path – I am so thankful for your support and that it led me here.

My beautiful parents Sharon and John Coburn, my brothers Matt and David, and my cousin Claire Allen, for their unconditional love and support.

All the pretty little horses – especially Spur, and my childhood buddy Stormy, who is in the great paddock in the sky.

Poetry – my heart and the reason I am here.

I would lastly like to thank Liv, most of all, for everything.